SEVEN SILLIES

Written by Joyce Dunbar

Illustrated by Chris Downing

Andersen Press · London

On a bright and shining morning Pig looked into the pond.

"There's a pig in the pond," said Pig.
"Such a handsome pig!"
And Pig called over to Sheep.

"What do you see in the pond?" asked Pig.
"I see a pig and a sheep," answered Sheep.
"Such a beautiful sheep!"
And Sheep called over to Goat.

"What do you see in the pond?" asked Sheep.
"I see a pig and a sheep and a goat," answered
Goat.
"Such a gorgeous goat."
And Goat called over to Rabbit.

"What do you see in the pond?" asked Goat.
"I see a pig and a sheep and a goat and a rabbit,"
answered Rabbit.
"Such a splendid rabbit!"
And Rabbit called over to Hen.

"What do you see in the pond?" asked Rabbit.
"I see a pig and a sheep and a goat and a rabbit
and a hen," said Hen.
"Such a fine feathered hen."
And Hen called over to Mouse.

"What do you see in the pond?" asked Hen.
"I see a pig and a sheep and a goat and a rabbit and a hen and a mouse," said Mouse.
"Such a dear little mouse."
And Mouse called over to Frog.

"What do you see in the pond?" asked Mouse.
"I see seven sillies," answered Frog.
"Seven sillies?" asked the pig and the sheep
and the goat and the rabbit and the hen and
the mouse. "What do you mean?"

"They are all in the pond and they want to get out," said Frog.
"How can we get them out?"
"You will have to jump in and fetch them," answered Frog.

So the pig and the sheep and the goat and the rabbit and the hen and mouse all jumped into the water with a splash!

"There is nothing in the pond after all!" they said.

"Oh yes there is," laughed Frog.
"There is a handsome pig,
a beautiful sheep,
a gorgeous goat,
a splendid rabbit,
a fine feathered hen,
a dear little mouse,
and that makes seven sillies."

The animals scrambled out of the pond all sopping wet and dripping with water. They did feel very silly!
"How many sillies?" asked Pig.

"Seven," answered Frog.
"Are you sure?" asked Pig.
Pig began to count. The animals joined in.
"One, two, three, four, five, six –"
The only one left was Frog.
"Aha!" they laughed. "SEVEN SILLIES!"

"We see a frog that can't count," they said.
"Such a foolish frog!"

For John and Kate Tremain - *J.D.*

For Caroline, Chloë and Max - *C.D.*

Text copyright ©1993 by Joyce Dunbar. Illustrations copyright ©1993 by Chris Downing.
This paperback edition first published in 2001 by Andersen Press Ltd.
The rights of Joyce Dunbar and Chris Downing to be identified as the author and illustrator
of this work have been asserted by them in accordance with the Copyright, Designs and Patents Act, 1988.
First published in Great Britain in 1993 by Andersen Press Ltd., 20 Vauxhall Bridge Road, London SW1V 2SA.
Published in Australia by Random House Australia Pty., 20 Alfred Street, Milsons Point, Sydney, NSW 2061.
All rights reserved. Colour separated in Switzerland by Photolitho AG, Zurich.
Printed and bound in China.

10 9 8 7 6 5 4 3 2 1

British Library Cataloguing in Publication Data available.

ISBN 0 86264 363 5

This book has been printed on acid-free paper